SURVIVAL OF THE ELEMENTS

THE STORY OF XAVIER KEY

MATTHEW ALBREN

ISBN: 1494822849
ISBN 13: 9781494822842

ACKNOWLEDGMENTS

I would first like to thank my parents for giving me this wonderful opportunity to publish my writing for the world to see. They, as well as my entire family, have been behind me the whole way as I begin my journey as a writer. I especially want to thank my brother, Adam, for finding creative ways to help me break away from my laptop so I could take time to refocus.

Next, I want to thank all of my writing teachers from elementary school who taught and supported me throughout the years: Mrs. Cronin, Mrs. Estella, Mrs. Foster, Ms. Stewart, and Dr. Rains. As far as my middle school teachers, I want to especially thank Ms. Hamel for being the first person ever to read the original story of Xavier Key and to be the first to edit it too. And Mrs. Bedell because she was the teacher who showed me the picture of a desert that kickstarted the life of Xavier Key and his world. Also, thanks to my current English teacher, Mr. Morris, who has given me some invaluable writing tips and encouraging words that

I will never forget. Lastly, thanks to Ms. Van Laethem, my Spanish teacher, whose different tips and tricks on how to look at life and handle tough situations have given me so many ideas on how to develop Xavier Key, Riley Aurarance, and also, myself.

Furthermore, thanks to all of my friends who have encouraged me along my writing journey and who have all helped in the development of my characters.

Lastly, thanks to all of the helpful team members at CreateSpace for their assistance in making my dream as a professional writer come true by editing, illustrating, and, of course, guiding me to publishing Xavier Key.

I hope you all enjoy reading about Xavier Key's adventures.

PROLOGUE

As a kid, I'd never understood why she'd covered my eyes. I thought that maybe I'd done something wrong, but how could a seven-year old playing with an uprooted dandelion do something wrong? I wouldn't understand for a few years. Now though, I am mature, older, and wiser. Now I understand that she'd done it because she hadn't wanted me to witness an event that would scar me for life.

Now that I'm twelve, it happened nearly five years ago. I'd been outside in the fields with my mother, a friend of hers, and her friend's daughter. The breeze had been unsettling that day, the kind that sends a chill racing up your spine, but I had ignored it and focused on the sun instead.

The fields were usually swamped with people, but today was a market day on our island, and people couldn't afford to miss those, so the fields were just long patches of freshly grown, great, green grass. I liked the fields because they were so vast and so free—an ocean of grass.

On that day, I'd found a small, lemony yellow dandelion, perfectly sized to fit in the center of my palm, protruding from the ground. I tugged on it for a few minutes as my mother sat in the grass and started a heated discussion with her friend, Ms. Brak. Her daughter, Sequoia, was really nice. Sequoia had long hair running passed her shoulders that reminded me of chocolate and her face was always creased with a smile. Sequoia was two years older than me, but we were still very close.

Eventually I yanked the dandelion out of the ground. Its stem was a little moist, but the smoothness was like cream. "Sequoia," I whispered in my chipper, little kid voice. "Come over here."

That was when it happened.

Sequoia skipped over and knelt beside me. She was wearing a plain pink t-shirt and jeans that were rolled up a little passed her ankles. Her chocolate hair was braided and ran down her back.

I showed her the dandelion and she smiled. "Pretty." She murmured. I was enjoying the little weed myself until my mother rose up and came to stand near me defensively. Her auburn hair was in a ponytail and her yellow sweater whirled in the wind. Ms. Brak, who wore overalls with pink streaks and a white t-shirt underneath, stood up too.

I looked where they were looking and spotted two people in black jackets advancing towards us. The two people wore black sunglasses, black gloves, black military boots, black pants, and both had a black baton hanging from their waist. They were meant to resemble men, but even as a little kid, I knew better. They were androids. Robots created to do the bidding of our ruler. They walked over to us and stood a few feet away.

The robot on the left spoke first, and strangely, its voice sounded perfectly human. "By demand of the Queen, there has been an order for a new handmaiden. A young hand-maiden." The robot nodded towards Sequoia. "Give us the girl, Sequoia Brak, and no one will be harmed."

At first, I didn't understand exactly what was going on, but everyone else seemed to.

My mother responded first, but there was more fear in her voice than confidence. "You may not have the girl. If the Queen insists on a new handmaiden, then I offer myself as replacement."

"No." Ms. Brak quickly intervened.

The android on the right spoke now, still staring hard at my mother. "Ma'am, your actions are disrespectful toward the Queen and the High Lord. As a citizen, you will do as you are told and give us Sequoia Brak." The android looked at Sequoia.

"Absolutely not! I will die first." My mother seemed to be hesitant because she didn't usually take charge, but Ms. Brak seemed paralyzed with fear, so my mother was the only one left to defend Sequoia.

"Easy to arrange." The left robot retorted smugly. Then it snapped its fingers. The robot on the right moved so fast, it was a blur. It grabbed Ms. Brak and held her arms down. She screamed and struggled, but could not escape.

"Get your hands off of me!" Ms. Brak shouted.

Then the left android lunged for Sequoia. My mother was fast though and used her entire body to shove the android down. Afterwards, she looked a bit dazed.

My mother pointed at me and then shouted to Sequoia, "Take him and run far away from here!" Sequoia nodded, but the left robot recovered too fast for any of us to react. It shot up like a bullet and grabbed my mother's right arm.

"Consequences are in order for not surrendering your daughter!" The mechanical creature bellowed angrily.

It drew its baton.

My mother fought hard to break free from the android's tight grip. "But, she's not my—" That was when Sequoia had cupped her hands over my eyes. In the moment where I was shocked and considered how to protest, I heard noises. There was something much like a baseball bat hitting a baseball, and I heard that more than once. At the same time there were blood-curdling shrieks ringing through my ears like an unstoppable church bell. They came from my mother.

That was when I tried to push Sequoia's hands away. "Sequoia, I can't see!" I whined. But her hand went limp and fell from my face anyway.

What I saw next was, to say the least, daunting. Seeing her sprawled out like that, like a dog had used her as a chew toy, her skin not only creamy white, but black and blue and brown too was horrific. I screamed and Sequoia grabbed me so my face could sink into her shoulder. Suddenly, the warm, sunny day was now just a distant memory.

"No!" Ms. Brak sobbed as she broke away from the right robot's grasp. "I'm Sequoia's mother, not her! Look what you've done fiends!"

The two robots looked down and seemed genuinely stunned. The left robot's voice did not waver when it spoke though. "Well then, will *you* hand over Sequoia Brak?"

"Never." Ms. Brak responded like it was too obvious. She gritted her teeth and balled her fists.

"Then you will face the same fate." The right robot announced. "Failure to obey the law results in punishment."

It raised its baton.

That was when Sequoia snatched my hand and began to run, causing me to drop my dandelion. We ran faster than I ever had in my life, our little legs carrying us over the flora. We just had to get away from there. Those demonic machines, they'd just done something that anyone would spend the rest of their life in prison for.

After running far enough away that the robots were nearly out of sight, we turned and looked back into the distance. The new crimson on the end of the robots' batons gleamed under the harsh glare of the sun and on the ground was my dandelion, although it lay crumpled as if it had been crushed with the ferocity of a bear.

I could tell Sequoia was trying hard not to cry. Her bottom lip was quivering and her eyes sparkled in the light because they were wet. "We should keep moving and get home." She choked on her words. "Your mother gave her life to save me. In return, I'll keep you safe. I promise."

We made our way through the waves of grass until we arrived back at civilization. People were bustling about. That was mostly because it was a market day, which was when everything at the market was on sale.

Two little kids walking around alone together must have looked strange, but no one cared enough to stop and ask if we needed help.

That was when my stomach churned. It wasn't the kind of *I have to throw up* churning or the anxious kind of churning either. It was rage. Anger. Hatred. It was the kind of bitterness that would never fade away. I hated just about everyone but Sequoia right then, but no one as much as the High Lord—no one as much as the man who'd indirectly orchestrated the death of my own mother.

TABLE OF CONTENTS

1

THE SILENCE OF THE RELEGATION CEREMONY

It was all silent. Everything as far as the eye could see or as far as the ear could hear was silent. Everyone was in wait. Palms were sweating, and everyone was standing straight, not saying a word. I looked in all directions, and I could only see a few boys among incredibly large numbers of women and girls. It was always like this when the Relegation Ceremony came. We'd all crowd together at the center of our island, shoulder to shoulder. We'd wait with bated breaths as the High Lord and his Queen prepared their speech. Every time I stood here, I knew that my time was going to come. After all, I was a boy, and boys were always eventually banished. And in any worse-case scenario, death could almost be ensured.

Our island was nothing special. One section was strictly limited to houses, which were more hut-like, round and made of straw, bound with tree sap and long, pliable wires. Nowadays, the portion of the island that was uncovered by houses was made up mostly of grain fields and maple trees, which were well tended by the citizens. The grass fields that used to cover a lot of space became less important once the grain fields prospered, so the grassy fields eventually yellowed and became nothing more than a wasteland soon forgotten by most of the people. The grain fields were larger than one would imagine and could, if necessary, provide enough food to feed almost the entire island. The maple trees simply provided wood.

The High Lord paid no attention to the trees, since he had his own private gardens, where trees and fruit-bearing plants were plentiful. Of course, I only know this based upon stories told by handmaidens that were relieved of duty or cast away by the Queen. Girls that were cast away were the ones she considered unnecessary and unworthy of a life as a citizen, so they would be offed within days for the simple entertainment of the Queen. In fact, a close friend of mine named Sequoia was forced to be a handmaiden for a brief amount of time, but the Queen ended up relieving her of duty soon after because she was too inexperienced.

When the Relegation Ceremony came, the High Lord made it mandatory for all citizens to leave their homes, regardless of personal or medical reasons, and show up to listen to the meeting. The High Lord warned us of awful consequences if a citizen were to miss such a meeting. However, I didn't know what the consequences would be, since no one in my lifetime had ever missed a Relegation Ceremony.

After an hour had passed in that awful, deep silence, I decided to sit down. I still didn't want to face that today was going to be my day, so I only let a blank stare wander across my face. Recently, when the date had been set, I'd figured it out and I had let the pain envelop me, but by now I knew I could only accept it. I had hoped that it wasn't true. I always had and always would. I didn't like it. The High Lord was never fair to his people.

I longed for someone to comfort me and tell me every-thing would be fine. I let my head fall forward a little bit. I was feeling the pain again—the pain of knowing that I was probably going to die.

I could swear I'd been sitting there for many long hours, but it must have been only a brief while later that the High Lord approached from his palace. He was a regal and ele-gant man. His face had wrinkled over many years of ruling. He had metallic-silver hair so spiky it looked as if it would cut anything that stroked across it, like porcupine quills. He was always serious: lips sealed, head high, back straight. His almost-sleepy eyes never focused on a citizen—to him, the citizens were clearly inferior. He took long strides and as he moved, the two red tails on his robe fluttered gracefully behind him. The way he walked, you'd think he was the king of the world.

The High Lord made his way to the center of the island so that all his people could gaze upon him. I kept my hands steady as I rose to my feet. The High Lord was motionless for a long moment, like something had triggered his "inner pause button" and held it down. Then, his eyes shot open as if something had just juiced them with life. They were like ice, and I could swear, that for a split second, he shot a dangerous, unforgiving glare at me.

2

BANISHMENT SPEECH

The High Lord had seen us all many times before, and yet, at every meeting, he took a long look at us all. I felt a droplet of sweat curl down my cheek and drip to the ground. I began to tap my hip with a shaky hand. I felt numb with fear. I guess I would've zoned out right about there, but I caught myself when something grasped my shoulder.

It was the Queen, making her way through the crowd. She wore a strict look on her face, and her blond hair was wavy like snakes. Her long, puffy dress was silver, with highlights of purple, red, and gold—and it made me think of a pool of shiny, hot blood. I felt a shiver run up my spine when she touched me, then a strange sensation. I closed my eyes and pushed out the feeling, then returned my blank stare toward the High Lord.

Once the Queen arrived at the High Lord's side, one of her handmaidens, dressed in a lime-green blouse and cream veil, placed a high, leather-covered stool by the Queen. The Queen pursed her lips, stared out at the crowd, and then sank onto her stool. The High Lord stayed on his feet.

I didn't know why, but I felt obligated to stay standing and pay attention.

The High Lord lowered his gaze, and his eyes began to wander across the notes that he held in his bony hands. Then, he turned to his Queen and whispered into her ear. When he moved his head away, the Queen closed her eyes for a moment, thinking. Then she shook her head, her wavy hair swinging, and then she patted her head, ensuring that her hair was still presentable. The High Lord nodded at her but seemed oddly dissatisfied. Then, the Queen clasped her hands together and waited silently for the High Lord to begin.

If something like that had happened on a regular day, people probably would've started murmuring, but today, no one dared to make a sound, no matter what thoughts crossed their minds. I felt the same way. The pain and anger that swam throughout my body could only keep swimming since I would not dare to speak. I kept my lips sealed and continued to focus entirely on the High Lord.

Finally, he looked down at his paper again, licked his lips, and opened his mouth to begin. I could feel my anxiety rising to a peak. I didn't want to hear anything the High Lord was about to say. I had enough in my head. But when he began, I listened anyway.

"Welcome all to yet another Relegation Ceremony," The High Lord began. Of course, I expected this part because the High Lord started every one of his speeches the same way. First, he would welcome us, describe the banishment standards, and name those who would be banished. Then it would get interesting.

He continued. "We have reached yet another six-month point. As you all know, every six months we meet for this semi-annual special meeting. Following tradition, I will now go over the banishment standards. As our society knows, all boys are taken away upon turning twelve years old so that they are not on our island during their early teen years. Boys have no overly important features because they work, they eat, and they sleep—they are unnecessary dead weight to our society. Girls, however, as we know, will be embraced by the loving arms of society. Girls can work, and their keen knowledge can also be useful. Girls understand important social issues like dress, trade, and food much better than boys. This is of course due to their natural likes and dislikes. However, girls cannot rule under any circumstances. The closest they can get is to marry the High Lord." The High Lord nodded at the Queen and she flashed a smile of perfectly straight white teeth as if to say *that's me everyone, the one and only, so enjoy me.*

The High Lord turned back to his paper and went on. "Now, as we all know, boys will become men who will be strong and possibly smart. These men may find it in themselves to desire the power I have as ruler. I will not take the risk of letting the High Lord be incompetent and that is why boys will be banished...or as I say, tested. Boys will be sent through a magical doorway to encounter the four major elements: earth, air, water, and fire. If a boy can survive in four elementally enhanced arenas and find his way back to the island, he will be accepted into society. Of course, the main reason for this test is that only a man as strong as I can ever rule the right way, and to be that strong, you must prove yourself and beat the test. So if a boy survives the test, returns, and challenges my rule, I will know that he is worthy. Or he may return and just simply be a citizen. But, with any luck, some of the boys here have some talent because, as we all know, there are no males living on our island right now that is above the age of twelve."

The High Lord stopped and took a breath, his first during the speech. I was shocked that even though he had stopped, he didn't seem the least bit tired from that constant talking. I gasped since I realized I hadn't taken a breath during the whole first portion of the speech. I took a minute to breathe. I was exhausted from just listening. Like I said, I was very anxious. The High Lord coughed quietly into his hand and then, after straightening the little curve in his paper he had created by holding it too tightly, continued his speech. I felt ready to crawl into a hole and never ever come out.

"Yes, so as we know, the tradition must be followed now to see if any twelve year olds among us now are worthy of someday taking my place, or if they are even worthy of survival. Thanks to records from the Pool of Life, where children can be born, I have the list of names here of the boys who have reached the age of twelve in the last six months. Please listen carefully." The High Lord stopped for a moment, reached into a small pocket, and took out a folded piece of paper. I felt my anxiety increase like a tangible thing as the High Lord unfolded his paper. I gulped.

The High Lord began reciting names in no particular order. "Alexander Clemonts, Raymond Lupe-Jon, Lloyd Russell, Scott Jayne." I felt the world get smaller around me as each name was read and a head somewhere in the crowd fell. I figured those kids all felt the same way I was feeling. It was all happening so fast now. I stopped listening as the names kept coming. It hurt to hear so many, like someone injecting countless needles just for the fun of it. Then, finally, I looked up, as the final name was called. It rang inside me like a ceaseless alarm clock as my stomach sank. I let my head fall forward like before, this time only feeling pity for myself. The High Lord repeated the name, my name. "Xavier Key."

The High Lord, although he was cruel, gave everyone a moment to cope with what they had just heard. I'm sure most people had been expecting it, but still, everyone was silent, thinking about the young boys who were about to face a fatal journey. I could feel the pain inside me finally settling down. It had happened now. The most painful part of this whole meeting would be facing my fate. I guess, in a way, I had begun to accept it—only in the smallest way possible and only because there was no argument that I could make. I exhaled softly.

Then the High Lord carried on with his speech. "Now, children, I am sure most of you were expecting this fate, so please don't resist. You know that I will be forced to end your life right here, in front of everyone, if you fight it. Remember, not all is ever truly lost." I thought I heard a hint of sympathy in the old man's voice, but it died away quickly, if it was even there. "Now that you understand the general outlines of the test, I will explain the more specific details."

My heart skipped a beat. This was it.

"The first enhanced arena will be earth. You will be transported to a large, seemingly endless desert. You will be supplied with one canister of water and a dinner roll. If you survive, you will face the second enhanced arena, air. In the air arena, you will be transported to a very high altitude above the Earth's surface, where there will be a platform. Upon arrival, you will be attacked by darkness demons. You will be supplied with a dagger, sleep spray, and a rope. If you survive the fight with the demons, you will be transported to the third enhanced arena, water. You will be transported to the bottom of a large body of water, where you will have to find a way to return to the surface. You will be supplied with an air tank that will last you thirty-six hours, a protective shell, and a small knife. Most will not make it past the third enhanced arena due to the short time limit. But if you are worthy, you will find the way, which will bring you to the fourth and final enhanced arena: fire. I will give no further information about the fourth enhanced arena as it is so vile and terrifying that you children must experience it for yourself—if you make it there. So, in overview, Arena One tests your endurance, Arena Two tests your strength and fighting abilities, Arena Three tests your smarts, and Arena Four tests you." The High Lord breathed in silently. He stared at the crowd. We'd all heard this many times before, but it got more intense every time we heard it. And I could feel it like a boulder on my shoulders, because I knew that soon, I would be facing it all first-hand.

3

ENTERING THE VORTEX

The High Lord waited a moment before beginning dismissal. He ordered all women and girls to return to their homes and not to work, so that they could take a day to remember their beloved boys. He also ordered all boys in the community to go to work, as they needed to work much harder due to the obvious lack of men. Lastly, all of the banished boys were ordered to approach the High Lord's palace where the magical door was located, and if anyone in our community felt that it was necessary, they would be allowed five minutes with the banished boys. My mind told me to stay put, but I forced myself toward the palace. The only thing that kept me moving was the fact that I was not alone.

I was never too great with numbers, but I guessed that there were at least twenty-five boys in the group of the banished. We were led into a small courtyard that was sealed off with a large gate that was silver like a full moon. The grass in the courtyard was beautiful green, the shade of green that all plants should be colored. Small flower buds lined the outer edges of the courtyard and they all reached for the sun.

None of us really knew what was going to happen in this courtyard. I knew that I had heard the High Lord say that there was a door to the arenas, but there was no door here except for the entrance to the small courtyard.

Suddenly, a large group of woman and girls swarmed into the area. Some of the boys became cloaked in the endless shower of females, desperate to say goodbye one last time. I looked around, seeing if there was anyone that I knew, and that was when I saw her. A girl was wandering around, looking for someone. She had curly chocolate-colored hair that fell just past her shoulders. Her face was perfect with caring, easy green-like-the-courtyard-grass eyes, a nose that was shaped so smoothly, it could've been an angel's work, and lips that were highlighted by a light, yet beautiful gloss of pink.

"Sequoia!" I yelled. She whipped around and found me. She smiled like she had just found a needle in a haystack. Sequoia shared a hut with me, and we had known each other for a long time. Sequoia was like the older sister that I never had. We didn't always get along, but deep down, we'd always be close. Sequoia was fourteen, but she treated me like an equal.

"You know X, I'm a little hurt that you weren't looking for me." I smiled a tiny bit. She weaved her way to me and now that she was close, I could tell that she'd been crying. She wrapped her arms around me. I thought I heard her choke back a sob. "Did you see me at the Relegation Ceremony?" She asked.

"No."

"Good, because I couldn't hold myself together when I heard *him* say your name. No one deserves what's about to happen to you, especially someone like you, X."

I had to choke down the lump in my throat to keep from crying right at that moment. I felt weak physically, but knew that this was the time when I had to be strongest emotionally. I pushed myself hard to say more, "Sequoia, you'll do great things, I know it. Please don't let what's going to happen to me influence your life. You should try to, maybe, forget about me for your own good. It's what our mothers would want."

Sequoia stared at me like I was crazy. I hated when she stared at me like that. It made me feel like she could see right through me. And I knew she didn't like what I'd said.

"X, I know I'm a girl, but you should know by now that I'm no softie. I'm never breaking my promise. We are friends to the end and beyond." Then she winked, probably because she knew that did speak volumes to me.

I choked, but was able to make out what I wanted to say. "Goodbye Sequoia." An obnoxious sound suddenly boomed through the courtyard and a swarm of androids in official suites and tinted sunglasses began to force all of the people except the banished boys out by force. I noticed that all of the officials had large batons at their waists, weapons I was all too familiar with, so I took one last look at Sequoia as her bottom lip quivered and she started to blink back tears. Then a robot in a suit and sunglasses grabbed her right arm and began to haul her away like she was a rag doll. I looked down as a feeling of loneliness crept over me.

Then, I heard Sequoia's voice once more, clear and smooth like the song of a robin, "Stay strong X! I believe in you!"

I knew she believed in me, she always had, but hearing her say it gave me one moment of comfort. Then, she yelled out three last words before the official yanked her out of sight, "Catch you later!" And then she was gone. I pondered what she said for a moment.

"Catch you later." I whispered.

✳ ✳ ✳

We were not allowed to enter the palace through the front door. Instead, we had to walk right down to the basement through an old door on the side of the huge building.

The basement was disgusting. Cobwebs were everywhere; you'd think that they were some kind of common decoration here. I kept moving along with the other boys. The High Lord raced to the front of the pack and moved us along like a pro. Finally, we arrived at a blank wall at the back of the room. The High Lord tapped his hand against it and the wall slid back and away to reveal a small door. It was caramel-colored and looked like it had been built recently. The beauty of the door helped my heart to rise just a tad.

The High Lord spoke. "You will each be given a small pack. The pack will contain your supplies for Arena One:

a water canister and a dinner roll, as I said earlier. There will also be a piece of paper inside that I strongly suggest you read. Furthermore, you will also be given a bag with the proper attire for Arena One, attire that you will be required to wear. Before each arena you will be given a new pack with the proper supplies and the correct attire to change into. Now, you must all change your clothes, then return to this door, get your pack, and walk on through. Anyone who resists, or does not desire to try and take his chances in the arenas may be immediately taken away and put to death. Any questions?" The High Lord did not waste more than a second waiting for an answer. "No? Good."

I picked up a neatly folded pile of clothes and made my way to a dark corner of the basement. I quickly changed my clothes and walked back toward the door. There was a mirror on the wall near the door and I glanced at it to see what my Arena One outfit looked like. I was wearing a silver vest over a white T-shirt and baggy beige pants. We hadn't been given shoes, so I was barefoot, which was unexpected, but I wasn't going to complain. In the quick second I had, I smoothed down my now ruffled dark hair, not that it really mattered.

Then, I spotted a small bucket with a label that read, "Leave clothes here," so I dumped my old clothes into the bucket. I frowned. I had liked that shirt, but I moved forward and a soldier handed me a pack. My pack was a light blue color with yellow designs that might have been meant to be birds and trees, obviously representing nature. I thought it was interesting how they designed something so nice that would either fry in the sun, get taken by demons, disintegrate underwater, or maybe even worse.

I gulped as I approached the door. I felt as though with every tiny step I took, the door leapt closer and closer to me like a tiger closing in on its feeble prey. My hands instantly began to sweat and my legs wobbled a bit. I held onto my pack tightly, squeezing it as though it were a newborn's first stuffed animal, as I pulled the door open to reveal a giant green-and-black vortex. There was no end to it. My stomach swirled and I noticed that my tongue was dry and I was parched.

The awfulness that I always knew would come with this day seemed to multiply rapidly as I realized that this was reality and this was my fate. That door held my fate inside, caging it, keeping it away, until I entered.

I looked back one more time. No one was behind me. I was the first to go. Perhaps I could've taken more time, but I couldn't do anything about it now, the High Lord had his eyes locked on me.

I faced the vortex once more and I felt my stomach flip again as I walked toward it. I closed my eyes and my life flashed before me: my childhood, my friends, my work, and the relentless hours I'd spent thinking about this moment, so I jumped in, tired of waiting to die, and as I did, I felt myself disappearing, melting.

The last words I heard were from the High Lord, who yelled, "Good luck, if you are truly worthy! And if not, then may you find peace with death."

4

BEGINNING ARENA ONE

I was sure that the pressure around me increased and decreased as I flew through the vortex. I dared not open my eyes for fear of passing out. I felt like I was on a bullet train that was reaching unknown speeds; it was such a rush. The vortex coaster, which is a name I can personally take credit for, lasted about a minute or so before I thought I stopped moving. I opened my eyes when my bare feet sank into warm sand.

I opened my eyes but quickly shut them again. The sun glared at me, and I wasn't expecting it. The warmth was nice and relaxing for the first few seconds, but then I began to sweat absurdly, unnaturally. The heat was overwhelming to say the least. I gasped. I dropped my pack and choked. The air was insanely dry, and my lungs hadn't adjusted. I coughed like a maniac; feeling like someone had stuffed a thorny bush down my throat and then decided to follow it up with a blast from a flamethrower.

Once I got my act together, I wiped away the drool that had pooled on my chin. Then I reached into my pack and pulled out the water canister. It was surprisingly small, about the size of an average tube of toothpaste. I gasped again. "What?" I yelled out, but I choked on the dry air.

After I recovered, I stared at the little canister and scowled. I unscrewed the cap and looked inside. At least it was filled to the rim, or I might have lost control of myself right there. I took a tiny sip, enough to calm my throat, but only as much as I needed. Then I screwed the cap back on and placed the canister back in my pack. Now that my eyes had adjusted, I could look around.

Imagine a beach, but force the sand to cover the water as far out as you can see and beyond, and then you might be able to imagine what I saw. It was all desert. No matter how you looked at it, I was smack dab in the center of the desert. The golden sand glistened against the sun and it might've seemed beautiful, if it wasn't intimidating.

I picked a direction at random and began to trudge along. I knew I was supposed to be looking for a passageway to Arena Two.

My feet sank into the sand with every step I took. That was when I understood why I was sent into Arena One barefoot. It was no gesture of thoughtfulness because the sand was scorching hot.

That was when I knew the torture was only just beginning.

✳ ✳ ✳

I walked for what could have been about twenty minutes, and nothing changed. I was still surrounded by sand. It was all sand; there weren't even any cacti around.

At that, I began to wonder if the arenas sustained plant life when I saw giant sand dunes in the distance. I was happily surprised when I realized that those sand dunes would probably make for a nice place to stop and rest. I began making my way toward them.

Once I arrived at the dunes, I plunked myself down in front of one so I was facing away from the sun.

I just needed to sit and breathe. The air seemed slightly more moist here than where I had entered and I was thankful for that.

I looked into my pack and pulled out the water canister and the dinner roll. The roll was larger than a roll usually is, at least three times larger than an average one. Perhaps the High Lord should've described the rolls as tiny loaves. The roll was very smooth in my hands and was mostly white, with a hint of crispy brown here and there.

I flushed my throat with another sip of water and supplied my stomach with a small slice of dinner roll, which turned out to be made of sourdough and was pretty crunchy, but delicious nonetheless.

Then I realized something.

The door with the vortex that had taken me here hadn't been behind me when I'd landed. That was strange. I wondered about it for a little while, pondering if the vortex had been an illusion. I had kept my eyes closed the entire time, but the ride seemed too real. I guess I'd have to hope I would get another chance to check.

Then something else came to mind.

I remembered that the High Lord had put a piece of paper in everyone's pack and he had advised reading it.

I looked up to see that the sun was beginning to set. It was later than I thought. I scrambled to pull the paper out. I would only have so much time to read it, all based on the glow of the sun.

I rapidly tried to find it, and in my careless rush, I accidently knocked my dinner roll into the sand, which was depressing. I scowled and brushed it off before placing it back into my pack.

Then I spotted the piece of paper.

I reached for it and pulled it out into the fading sunlight. The paper was smooth and light, like a bird's feather, and I could tell that whoever had crafted it had put lots of effort into make it perfect. It was written on in beautiful, crisp, black ink. There were miniature golden designs running around the edges. I scanned it quickly, and then read it word for word.

Dear Banished Boy,

You have now passed through the vortex, and I see you were smart enough to take out my note. This note will help you survive, I assure you. Hidden within each arena are five powerful orbs called pulses. Each pulse has its own unique elemental property. If you find these pulses and take them with you, they will give you strength and protection when you need it, as well as stop any need for food or water, as they will give you the necessary energy. They are not my creation, and their true purpose is unknown. Listed below are the pulses and where they are found.

Earth	Air	Water	Fire
Rock Pulse	Flying Pulse	Water Pulse	Heat Pulse
Earth Pulse	Sky Pulse	Freeze Pulse	Fantasy Pulse
Metal Pulse	Darkness Pulse	Bubble Pulse	Poison Pulse
Combat Pulse	Shadow Pulse	Confuse Pulse	Snooze Pulse
Scorch Pulse	Air Pulse	Creation Pulse	Destruction Pulse

Good luck if you are truly worthy! And if not, then may you find peace with death.

—The High Lord

I read and reread the note until the sun had disappeared.

I wanted to cheer. If I found these supposedly magical pulses, then I might survive. They would protect me. I was happy for a long moment, and then I frowned.

The note said they were hidden, and frankly, I could not spend my days searching for magical orbs that might not even be near me. I understood that I could not survive alone though. That would be madness. Still, I decided right there that my goal was not to find the pulses, but that I would look for them while I pushed on to survive.

5

DISCOVERING THE SCORCH

A whole night must have passed before I realized I had fallen asleep on the warm sand. I hadn't meant to doze off. Losing time in any arena could mean death, but I was just tired, overwhelmed—and preoccupied with the pulses.

I couldn't stop thinking about them. There were twenty pulses. I knew there was nearly no chance of me ever finding one, but my mind rushed with the thought. I just had to put the pulses in the back of my mind though because I had decided that I was here to survive, not to go treasure hunting.

The sun was blazing yet again today. It might've been hotter than when I arrived now, but I was numb to the heat and couldn't honestly tell for sure.

After a quick swig of water, I started walking again. I walked for what I judged to be approximately thirty minutes, but it felt more like sixty.

Everything was slow in Arena One since there was no finish line in sight. I may as well have been walking on a treadmill. In fact, I couldn't even say I knew what I was looking for.

I longed for a clue of some sort. I felt as though my existence was getting more and more worthless by the minute, and I was growing lonelier and more tired.

I pulled out my canister of water while I walked. The water had begun to get warm, but even warm, it still tasted cool and refreshing. I swallowed a huge gulp before screwing the cap back on and placing it back in my pack.

I had definitely been walking for hours now; my exhaustion was a sure sign. It was also nearing nighttime, and there were no sand dunes in sight, not like last night.

I really didn't want to sleep flat on the sand. I wanted to keep moving and find the doorway. But after about three more hours of walking I was overcome by my exhaustion. I fell face-first into the sand and slept for a long time.

When I woke up, my face was caked with sand, as was my whole body, and the sand had a giant imprint of my body in it. I knew if Sequoia were here, she would've said something she thought was witty about making a "sand angel" but not even that was enough to make me smile.

I dusted myself off. The sun was glaring at me, as expected, taunting me by spitting unbearable heat my way.

Now that it was day three, I was beginning to understand that this whole arena idea was no small challenge. I hated admitting it, but this really was forcing my physical and mental abilities to the maximum.

I patted down my stomach, which was hissing wildly, snake-style, when I realized that I hadn't taken my dinner roll out since the first night. I shoved my hand into my pack and fished it out. I was flabbergasted to find that there were only a few bites left, and I hadn't touched the thing in days. My hungry stomach growled uneasily.

I was absolutely stunned. I hadn't seen one living creature at all since I'd arrived here. What could've happened to my dinner roll? Someone or something had been eating it. I wanted to scream and yell and rip my hair out, but I was the only thing around for miles, so my animal-like rage wouldn't do much good.

I looked down as the wave of loneliness swept over me again.

I decided that tonight I would not fall asleep.

I was going to stay up for the whole night and catch whoever was making a feast of my dinner roll.

When the sun set once again on day three, I plopped down in the sand and sat silently with my legs crossed.

I placed my pack behind me like a pillow, and I lay down so I could gaze up at the stars. There were more than I had imagined. I hadn't even thought to look at the stars until now. They had a soft glow that made me feel all warm and tingly inside.

After carefully studying the night sky, I found what I was looking for.

The constellation Columba was in sight. When I was very little, my mother had taught me how to find Columba because it was the Dove, a symbol of hope. My mother had said that if I was ever lost I should wait until nightfall, find Columba, and it would offer me hope.

Well, I'd never been as lost as I was right now.

Something incredible—something impossible—happened right at that moment.

The sand began to dissolve below me and around me. It all dissolved into the ground as though a drain had sucked it up, leaving a floor of metallic tiles extending for miles in all directions.

I gasped and stood up. What was happening?

I pulled out the note the High Lord had written. I stared at it as the idea of the pulses rushed back into my mind. This was all incredibly sudden and supernatural, but I thought for once I actually had some hope.

This was no random happening.

I looked once again at the list of pulses under "Earth." I read them aloud, "Rock, Earth, Metal, Combat, and...Scorch."

Scorch.

The word ran through my head a couple of times. It sounded familiar in a vague sort of way. I eyed the words, and again I paused at "Scorch." Then I recalled the word. I had read about it in a book once. It meant *to burn a surface, or to dry or shrivel using intense heat.*

I stood bewildered for a moment, as the blank, metal plain around me seemed to continue expanding. I began to walk across the tiles slowly. They were cool against my feet, like walking across an unused, metal vent. I kept walking.

Then, all of a sudden, a monument rose up right in front of me from out of nowhere. Then another monument popped up behind me—then one to the left and one to the right. Four pillar-like monuments. I stared at them.

On each there was a powerful-looking engraving.

I read each engraving aloud. "The hard substance of which that is rock. Swallowing itself down in its own rivers that is earth. A solid of steel that is metal. To bring it upon with strength that is combat." I began to understand that these pillars must somehow be connected to the pulses in Arena One.

I figured since the writing was so strange, it might have been written by the ancients.

Then I realized that one monument was missing—one to represent scorch. Before another thought could entangle me, the monuments began to glow feverishly. I covered my eyes just a bit to defend against the bright light.

Then, in front of each monument, green rays of light shot down, and within each one was a glowing orb, about the size of a baseball, or perhaps slightly larger.

Could it be true?

Were these the actual pulses that the High Lord had written about in his letter?

The rock pulse was brown with amber streaks; the earth pulse was more wood-like and rustic; the metal pulse was silver all over; and the combat pulse was orange with golden streaks in it. I stared at them all. They were surely a sight for sore eyes. I reached for the Metal Pulse but when I touched it, sharp prickles ran up my arm causing me to lurch away rapidly.

All of a sudden, a green ray of light shot down from up above and surrounded me.

I gasped as a small golden-orange orb with glossy red and pink tints floated gently toward me from above. I reached for it, and unlike the Metal Pulse, this one landed softly in my hands. Its smoothness and roundness was warm in a comforting sort of way.

"The Scorch Pulse," I breathed.

The Scorch Pulse felt just right in my hand, as though it were meant to sit on my palm forever. It was far more beautiful than all of the others. I reached for my pack and slipped the pulse inside. This was the first step—my first step toward a true chance at survival.

6

THE DARKNESS DEMONS RISE

My pack was heavier now with the added weight of the Scorch Pulse, but I didn't mind. I kept moving along.

After I had collected the Scorch Pulse, the tiles disappeared and I slept for a long time. When I woke up, I thought I had been dreaming, but sure enough, the Scorch Pulse was still with me, sitting silently at the bottom of my pack.

The desert had returned, and I was still lost and walking aimlessly. I reached for the Scorch Pulse from my pack and stared at it. "You must have some clue for me," I muttered in an imploring tone. But, unfortunately, the pulse did nothing.

I was more tired now than ever before, stopping often to clutch my stomach or try to learn how a person swallowed without choking. I'd never faced such a challenge as this. Running through the market trying to find exotic spices was one thing, but Arena One was like running through the market when the exotic spices were unavailable; it's pointless, exhausting, and makes you mad. So, even though I had only just begun walking, I stopped and plunked down in the sand. It was very hot, scorching even, and made me tense uncomfortably for a moment as the heat curled around my legs. I placed the Scorch Pulse beside me and I closed my eyes.

When I opened them, the Scorch Pulse was glowing feverishly with a red light, as though it had just cleared its throat and was trying to say something.

Now, the Scorch Pulse was incredibly hot to the touch, like an overheated stove. I couldn't hold onto it for more than a few seconds before flinging it down to try and fight the searing pain on my skin.

That didn't matter though, because the pulse began to move on its own.

It rolled along through the sand at breakneck speed, like an armadillo at a coyote gathering. It was fast and I had to run to keep up with it, so coughing and wheezing was inevitable.

Once the Scorch Pulse stopped rolling, we were still in the middle of the desert. The only difference now was that a long trail of human footprints was laid out behind me.

I looked around expectantly.

The pulse stopped glowing.

I stared at it in disbelief. Had it brought me here for no reason at all? I was so confused, so wrapped up in thought.

Then, before my eyes, a hole, a tornado-shaped pit, began to form in the ground. It began to whirl around and

I looked into the opening. The sight shocked me. There it was!

A green and black vortex!

"This is it!" I yelled as the wind from the vortex teased my hair. I scooped up the Scorch Pulse and jumped into the huge vortex, not once looking back at Arena One.

* * *

When I landed, a cool breeze greeted my face. My eyes shot open. I had arrived in Arena Two, finally! I was thrilled for a moment—before I looked around.

Unlike Arena One, where I had time to take it all in, here, before I could even figure out where I was, a long claw swiped at my face. I leapt back in fear and fell down.

I was being attacked by a creature.

And then I gasped in terror and astonishment.

It wasn't one creature that was attacking me. It was creatures! Millions of them. They were completely black as a midnight sky all over with long, hooked claws extending from their hands and feet. They had small, black-feathered wings flapping up and down on their backs. And they were about half a foot taller than me. But their faces were the most horrifying. Their mouths were all teeth, and they looked razor-sharp, like butcher knives. Their noses extended forward in what seemed like an uncomfortable sort of way, like they were too big for their faces. And their eyes...oh, their eyes. The most revolting part of them. They were egg-shaped and dark, sickly green like old moss.

I was extremely disgusted to the point where, if I'd had the energy, I would've puked. But I didn't have much time to think about it because a claw latched onto the back of my shirt, hoisted me up, and flung me down again, hard and onto my stomach, forcing the wind out of me.

I cursed under my breath in pain, and then I realized that my chin was coated with blood. I raised myself up on my elbows and glanced around. There were so many creatures.

And then, I remembered the High Lord's words. *In the air arena, you will be transported to a very high altitude above the Earth's surface. There, you will be attacked by darkness demons. You will be supplied with a dagger, sleep spray, and a rope.*

I quickly stood and stumbled backward. My legs were sore and felt like lead. It was bizarre no longer feeling the hot sand underneath my feet, but they felt stiff and padded.

I looked down. I had combat boots on. I scanned my whole body. My outfit had changed. I was now in a black shirt marked with an X in its center, perfectly fitted jeans, and combat boots. I was in an outfit that would make fighting easy enough that I wouldn't get killed immediately.

I looked again at the darkness demons; they were acting like bees, all swarming together, preparing or plotting, and intimidating me. I reached for my pack now, and for the first time, I realized it had gained weight. "How much happens on a vortex coaster?" I wondered aloud.

I had a split second while the demons readied themselves for an assault so I glanced into my pack. It now held a miniature dagger that had a violet sheath encasing its blade and a small hilt that looked easy to grip with its layers of banana yellow wrappings, a small, neon pink bottle of what was presumably sleep spray, and a long, thick, coiled rope. The Scorch Pulse rested on top of the rope, glowing softly.

I grasped the dagger in my hand and found that it was very light, about the weight of a banana, but it didn't feel like it fit my hand the right way, as if the shape of the hilt was never meant for my hand, and I decided that this could not have been an accident.

Right then, I remembered the High Lord's other words. *If you survive the fight with the demons, you will be transported to the third arena, water.* I was going to need to survive the fight with the demons. I readied myself by freeing the dagger's blade from its sheath, letting its metallic silver shine gleam, ready for a fight.

Almost instantly, a darkness demon lunged at me, shrieking like a banshee. It was a menacing noise that made me want to crawl under a table and hide. I quickly brought up the dagger as a form of defense, but I only sliced through air as an unexpected kick bashed into my chest, hurtling me backward. I landed with a thud.

My back ached from that landing. I got up again, but instantly, two large claws slashed at me, making the X on my shirt disappear and leaving my skin exposed. It was a perfect cut, but I knew I was now very vulnerable. I reached for my pack, but a demon wrapped its claw around my pack and lifted it away. I gritted my teeth.

Then another demon shoved me forward from behind with all its might and I lost my balance. I went flying forward, sliding along the ground, until I fell over an edge, which I only just caught with my fingertips.

I clung to the platform, dangling down from it, and my hands started to feel slippery with sweat.

I looked down where miles below was Earth's surface. Now the High Lord's words all made sense. I was literally fighting the demons on a platform in the sky.

I was hanging on for dear life—and I was mortified. A darkness demon landed above me and kicked at my unprotected face.

I had never been in so much pain in my life.

The demon threw out kick after kick and every direct hit left my vision blurred more and more. My nose began to pour blood. I yelled in agony, as if someone was slowly breaking each of my fingers at the pace of a snail.

Then, two demons swooped down below me and started swiping at my legs with their claws.

I was in so much pain that I was ready to let go and fall to my end. I decided death would be a whole lot better than this pain.

But seconds before I fell, a small figure, definitely a human, tackled the demon that was kicking my face with the force of a rhinoceros.

I was no longer being attacked, but I still couldn't pull myself up. I felt numb, and I was choking on the blood sliding into my mouth. Then the figure grabbed my arm and hoisted me up with surprising force. I was stunned.

It was a boy.

I couldn't tell if he was my age or not; he was really short. I looked at him, and he looked at me, and I felt as though he wanted to say something, but then two darkness demons swooped down and lifted the boy high into the air with their claws.

The boy struggled mightily, but couldn't escape.

"No!" I yelled in my now-raspy voice, which had clearly suffered from being idle. The demons whirled around and sent the boy tumbling to the platform's surface.

He landed hard.

I bit my tongue to suppress a scream and then raced to help him. I was empty-handed, alone, and defenseless with my life on the line, and yet, I found myself running at top speed to help the boy who had helped me.

But before I could get to him, a large darkness demon, bigger than most of the others, drove its claws into the boy's stomach. I heard him gasp the way a balloon does when it expels air. Then my pack came flying at my head and knocked me unconscious, just inches away from the only other human being for miles around.

7

ESCAPING WITH RILEY

Based on the dimness of the light, I guessed that I'd been out for many hours. I was weak, my muscles were sore, and my head was pounding madly. At first, I was groggy when I woke up, and then it all came flooding back to me. The boy. The boy who had saved me from those vicious demons. What had happened to him?

I tried to roll over and realized my hands and ankles were tied together with thick, coarse rope. The rope was the material that is used on scratching posts and it caused my limbs to feel numb, a feeling I did not like. The demons must have struggled to tie me up with their claws because the knots were tight but terribly misshapen. I struggled to a sitting position and looked around. I was alone in a small room. The walls were bare and old; I felt as though I was trapped inside a crate. I leaned up against one of the walls for support. I wanted to stand up. But I soon found out that my muscles were weaker than I had originally thought. I figured that this was because I had used them so much in the past few days and then, since my body hadn't been operating at all for several hours, they must have stiffened, so I just sat there for a long time. Soon enough, I dozed off once more.

When I woke up again, I was in a different room. I stared around, hoping for some reassurance. I was in the center of the room and darkness coated the space from all angles. The knots that were around my wrists seemed tighter, but the knots around my ankles seemed looser than before, and my shirt was gone, leaving my bare skin exposed, which had lots of tiny red marks covering its surface. It was possible that it had just slipped off soon after the demon sliced it apart.

Suddenly, the door to the room opened, letting some light peek in, and the boy who had saved me stumbled in, as though a strong force had pushed him. I tried to stand up fast, but instantly fell forward because my legs wouldn't hold me. The boy fell to his knees too and he looked at me. He had long midnight black hair that hung over his eyes and curled back at his neck, reminding me of seaweed, and green eyes that gleamed faintly, reminding me of olives. His face had open cuts and very noticeable bruises all over it, and he looked weak. He was barefoot and without a shirt as well. There were deep claw marks in his stomach that were coated in dried blood. They looked incredibly painful, making me wince at just the sight.

The boy put on a brave face. "Hi," he murmured. I stared in shock. A real human being was speaking to me. It felt like ages since I'd had a conversation.

"Hello," I gasped.

"I guess I should introduce myself. The name's Riley. Riley Aurarance." The way that the boy spoke, with such ease and maturity, made me realize that he must be pretty smart.

"I'm Xavier Key."

"Xavier, huh?"

"Yeah, that's right," I thought about my next few words carefully, "You know Riley, if it weren't for you, I probably wouldn't be here right now, so thanks. You saved my life." Riley shifted his body to avoid eye contact with me, which I found strange. "What did I say?"

"...Nothing. It's just me. These knots are too tight for my taste," Riley suddenly seemed very uncomfortable, but I couldn't really understand what he was thinking yet. "It's not fair that a ten year old has to endure the vicissitudes of this awful, torturous, *test*." Riley pouted and he struggled to remove the ropes around his wrists to no avail.

"Wait a minute, you're ten?"

"Of course. Did you think that I was just naturally short?" If I had been carrying something fragile at that moment, I probably would have dropped it and broken it; I was utterly shocked.

"But kids aren't supposed to be banished until they're twelve right? Why are you out here? This is no place for a kid." It was weird saying this, since I was a kid too, but the difference in maturity between ten years old and twelve years old seemed very great to me, based on the situation.

"Xavier, there's a simple explanation for it, but you might find it hard to believe, if I tell you."

"Okay."

"I'm a good fighter."

"That's it? That's the reason? What does that have to do with anything?"

"It has to do with the High Lord and *his* throne. The High Lord is a sorry excuse for a ruler. He's a coward."

"I agree with you, but I don't understand how that puts a ten year old kid in the arenas."

"Xavier, everybody knows that the High Lord uses the arenas to test young boys and see if they are worthy of becoming men, right?"

"And to see if they could possibly take his throne, yeah. Everyone knows that pathetic story."

"The High Lord thinks I am a threat to his power. I'm not bragging when I say this, but I am an incredible hand-to-hand combat fighter, and do pretty well with a spear and shield too. The High Lord does not take risks, so he banished me two years early, to protect himself and his precious power from the possibility of me challenging it before I was banished." I thought about this for a moment, and took it all in. This only furthered my notion that the High Lord was a cruel tyrant.

"But being ten puts you at a huge disadvantage out here." I could feel myself taking pity on Riley, and for a moment it reminded me of how Sequoia had once treated me, and I smiled for a quick moment as her face flashed before me.

"You're right. I am at a great disadvantage. And that disadvantage is so great that the High Lord, or anyone else, may as well just call me dead already."

"Then that means, the High Lord sent you out here simply to—" I had to stop myself; I couldn't just say that to him.

"To die? Yes. I've come to accept it, so you can say it aloud." I had to sit and think about this for a long time. *To die*. The words kept running through my head. *To die*. They seemed like the only two words in the world at the moment, and this boy had found someway to accept them.

Riley confused me, and so did the High Lord. Then, Riley started to look around the room like a perspicacious cat; he was taking in every detail. His eyes wandered the walls, and suddenly, his eyes lit up and he smiled like a boy who had just won a game of hide-and-seek. "So that's where we are."

"You know where we are?"

"Yeah. See that symbol on the wall over there?" I looked where Riley had been looking and found the symbol, shocked that I hadn't noticed it before and I wondered how Riley had known that it was there. The symbol was faded, but I could tell that it was an image of two fangs colored a chalky burgundy.

"The fangs?"

"Yes. The fangs are the symbol of the darkness demons in Arena Two."

"We're still in the arena? How do you know that?"

"I'll tell you some other time. What you should know is that we're being held by darkness demons. If the demons can defeat boys passing through their arena the High Lord orders that the boys be held, not killed. This is because the High Lord believes that if a boy can't survive a legion of demons, he's not a worthy leader, and therefore his execution will be monitored by the High Lord himself."

The High Lord was coming to execute us. That made my stomach flip. I knew that our only hope was to escape. We'd have to do it together, because alone, we were powerless. Even worse, my pack, along with the Scorch Pulse, was gone.

I devised a plan that I was sure would get us out of there. I knew that the High Lord was coming to execute us personally, so we would have to be sneaky. I also knew we'd have to take a risk and rely on luck. I looked around again, this time straining to see my surroundings. It took a while, but I finally thought of a perfect plan using the darkness to our advantage. Riley said he liked it, and just like me, he wanted to escape, but he made a point that I hadn't considered, "As smart as that is, how would we move with these bothersome bonds binding our limbs together?"

"Good point. I didn't think of that. Maybe this plan won't work."

"Xavier, let's try before giving up. That plan seems crafty enough that we might just escape. I know that we've both tried to break through the rope ourselves, but what if we did it for each other? Here, give me your wrists." I held out my wrists and groaned. Riley raised his arms so that his elbows rested on his knees and he began to work on freeing me from my constraint. His hands felt like metal. They were icy cold and very raw. He began to exhale very loudly and his stomach made a sound like a tractor. Sweat was swimming down his face in waterfalls. I felt guilty inside when I realized that I should've been freeing Riley and not the other way around, seeing as he was two years younger than me. I bit my lip and was about to tell Riley to take a rest when he made a squealing sound. "There we go!" He exclaimed.

Riley grabbed my left wrist and pushed it gently so that my two hands touched. Then, he tugged on the rope around my right wrist and I felt like I was being reborn. The rest of the rope came undone and dropped to the floor. Riley had freed me and the feeling of my wrists being able to breath again was amazing. I rubbed them, getting my blood flowing again, and then Riley instructed me on how to free him.

In no time at all we were both completely emancipated, and then we were ready to begin my plan. We both scurried into separate corners of the room and waited.

It was a long, anxious wait, but the doors finally opened and white light from the outside hallway beamed inside. As the High Lord strolled in, two demons behind him, I was surprised to see the Queen saunter in with them. What was she doing here? I couldn't worry about it now. Quickly, I covered my face to lessen the sound of my breathing.

The High Lord and the Queen looked around. "Now, I know you demons here are fools, but are you really so idiotic that you could lose two obnoxious boys?" The High Lord's voice did not sound merciful. The demons both tilted their heads, shocked. They looked around, their bizarre green eyes wandering everywhere. I gulped silently. The High Lord began searching too. This was the chance we needed. We both leapt to our feet and raced out the open doors straight passed the Queen, leaving our adversaries completely overwhelmed.

The High Lord stuttered and then yelled, "After them! There they go!" The demons shrieked, and thousands of the nasty creatures instantly appeared behind us. Riley and I kept running. We turned corner after corner, knowing that we had to escape. Some demons began to fly after us; they were getting angry. I was exhausted now. My muscles ached like never before, but I pushed on, fueled by fear of the darkness demons, and by my hatred for the High Lord and his plans for my death.

8

MILES BELOW THE SURFACE

We made it outside. The air was moist and recharging. I ran after Riley, who was right in front of me. Demons flew at us from every direction, claws reaching for our bare skin. I could feel hundreds of claws scrape across my stomach and face. I kept moving though, never slowing my pace. Riley seemed very resistant to pain, and he moved even faster than me. I rushed to keep up with his small but speedy strides. I didn't know where we were going, but it seemed like Riley did, and I knew following him was my best shot at getting out of there. Then, glancing to my left, I saw a demon, and in its claw was my pack.

I needed that pack. I leapt into the air and swung myself onto the demon's back. It yelled and started to struggle. I reached for my pack, but the demon's claw was flapping around in a wild rage with the rest of its body. I had few options, so I bit into the demon's right wing with all my might.

Let me just say that I could have been the hungriest person in the world and the taste of feathers and demon flesh would still be utterly disgusting. It tasted like an undercooked turkey wrapped in a coarse blanket, but I kept clamping down harder.

Then, I rammed my fist into the demon's head. After only a moment, the demon fell out of the sky. I slipped off its back and grabbed my pack.

Riley was nowhere to be seen now. I looked around wildly, but a demon came at me from the right, catching me off guard. I fell back. But before I could finish my fall, a hand grasped my wrist. Riley was riding a darkness demon like a pro. "Hang on!" Riley shouted, and we went flying forward.

I saw Riley pulling on the demon's ears. I guess that was controlling its movement. Then, we did a nosedive over the edge of the platform in the sky. "Wait!" I yelled, terrified. Riley flipped off the demon in midair, still grasping my wrist. "Thanks for the ride!" he yelled, and then we fell toward Earth.

"RILEY!" I yelled. But before he could reply, we fell into a vortex, and Arena Two was history.

✳ ✳ ✳

I had not expected such a thing. Riley had known, somehow, that the ground below us was not really there. It was a simple illusion to fool idiots like me who didn't want to fall all that way.

Riley had saved me again. I was grateful for a moment.

But then, I grew angry. Had he not "helped" me before, I could've blown through Arena Two. But it didn't really matter now since I was on my way to Arena Three.

When ride number three on the vortex coaster was over, I felt very squished, like there was a pressure increase. I opened my eyes to an amazing sight; I was underwater! I had an air tank strapped over my shoulders that was resting on my back and I had a timer strapped around my wrist that read 35:49—the amount of air that I had left. That made me shiver. Next, I discovered a pair of black headphones with a small microphone jutting out of the left side of them resting on my head. Why I had them, I didn't know. Then I noticed my pack. It was different now. It had a clear, protective shell around it that was apparently resistant to water, but I could still reach inside it. When I flipped the pack open, I saw that the Scorch Pulse was safely inside, but there was a small knife at the bottom of my pack too. Then, I noticed something that would've been hard to pick up on without a keen eye: I too had a protective shell surrounding me, just like my pack (I'd be wondering why my clothes weren't at all sodden). I could only tell because my shell had a faint, yet shiny, purple glow outlining it. It was neat, but I could not feel it. It must have been pushing away the water pressure and protecting me from getting absolutely soaked. And, the air from the air tank must've been getting trapped in the shell so that I could use it. As I was thinking about how the used air was being expelled, I realized I was missing something important, something I came here with—Riley.

I looked around. Bubbles drifted away from my shell. The water was amazingly clear. I could see coral the color of limes and plums and fish that sparkled like stars, but no Riley. Then, as if by magic, Riley crashed into me as he was thrown out of the vortex coaster. The water around us cushioned the collision, but it still caught me off guard. Riley was wearing the same outfit as me—a plain, yellow t-shirt and jeans with a purple-outlined encasement, an air tank, and a headset with a microphone. I saw his mouth begin to move, and somehow, I heard him. "I guess you got out of the vortex before me." I nodded my head.

"How can I hear you?" I asked Riley.

"The headsets are connected wirelessly since we're so close to each other." I had never felt so stupid. Duh! The headset! I shook my head and smirked.

"Well now that I've asked you to explain the obvious," I chuckled, "How about explaining the unobvious?"

"If you're wondering about the shell, it's meant to do exactly what you'd expect underwater. It relieves pressure so you don't get squished to death, it constantly takes in oxygen from the air tank so that you can breathe, and it shields against liquid substances."

"That's what I figured."

"And," Riley continued, "The timer on your wrist is counting down your hours of oxygen." I looked at the timer on my wrist and now it read 35:38. Time was going by too quickly.

"We should really get moving," I said. I really didn't want a watery grave. I looked around again. Now that I had survived two arenas, I was feeling more confident, but there was no sign of an exit from under the water. I knew this would be a tough one. Reaching the surface from miles below it could be the hardest task I would ever face.

I stumbled about foolishly as Riley and I moved along. It took lots of effort to keep moving underwater by paddling and swimming. Riley, on the other hand, seemed very confident in every movement he made. He acted without fear, as if nothing could hurt him. That made me wonder. He was so young, and yet, he seemed a lot better at this whole "survival thing" than me. I looked Riley up and down. I couldn't see his pack. I reached out and tapped his shoulder. He looked at me, startled. I held up my pack, pointed at it, and then pointed at him with one hand raised as if to imply a question. He waved his hand gently through the water, and suddenly, there it was! His pack just appeared. It was startling and caused me to stumble back. He reached for it and then held it out to me. I gripped it, but before he let go, I asked, "How'd you do that?"

Riley stared at me for a moment and hesitated before answering. "My dad taught me that trick." Then he whipped around and began paddling away. I stared at him. His dad? I wondered what he'd meant by that. I shook my head. I started moving again, fast so I could keep up with Riley, but I stopped dead in my tracks when I looked into his pack. Deep within it was not only a small knife, but also two, small, delicate orbs.

9

A DREAM TIED TO DESTINY

My eyes widened in shock. Was I seeing things? Did Riley actually have two pulses? I looked up to seek out Riley. He was facing away with his back turned to me. I stared in amazement. "Riley, you never mentioned that you had pulses. Where did you get them? Which ones are they?"

Riley turned around, glaring at me, and he snatched his pack away. I was surprised at Riley's reaction. He'd seemed so easy and calm and collected before. He turned around and continued moving through the seemingly endless water without saying a word. I chased after him as quickly as I could. "Riley! Wait!" I yelled. "Wait!" Riley stopped moving. I almost crashed into him but caught myself. I exhaled. "If it makes you feel any better, I have one of the pulses too."

Riley whipped around, a movement that looked very strange as the water resisted his quick movements. "I—you're lying! That's impossible!"

I raised an eyebrow. "Hold on." I opened my pack carefully, as though it were a Christmas gift, and revealed the Scorch Pulse to Riley. He stared at it like he'd never seen one before. His jaw dropped.

"You—but how is that possible?" I could see his nose twitch as he reached into his pack. He held out the two pulses to me so I could get a better look at them. One of them I instantly recognized from Arena One—the Combat Pulse. It was still a lovely shade of orange, and the golden streaks running through it made it strongly resemble the Scorch Pulse. That also explained why Riley was such a good fighter. His connection with the Combat Pulse must have been strong from the very beginning. But the other one was unfamiliar. It was translucent. From what I could see, the pulse was a light shade of purple with sharp black indentations constantly appearing, disappearing, and reappearing all over it. I wanted to reach out and touch it, but I resisted.

"Which pulse is that one?" I asked.

Riley looked at the Combat Pulse, and I shook my head. "Oh, this one?" he asked pointing to the purple one. "It's called the Shadow Pulse. I discovered it in Arena Two." That was when it hit me. I had never found the pulses in Arena Two, even though I had found them in Arena One.

"Riley," I said, "If we both discovered a pulse within Arena One, why didn't I find a pulse within Arena Two?"

Riley stared at me again, wondering about the question for a brief moment, his eyes flickering. "It's quite simple actually. See, to find a pulse you must have a connection to it at birth. That is what the High Lord leaves out of his letters. You won't know until you actually begin your banishment test, and of course, you won't know what pulse you're connected to either. But most people have no special connection to the pulses, and they are invisible to those who weren't born with the ability to see them. I guess you and I were both born special. The only reason you didn't come across the pulses in Arena Two is because you had no connection with any of them. That doesn't mean you won't see the pulses here in Arena Three or in Arena Four." Riley stopped and took a breath.

"You're very smart you know," I commented.

"Yeah, I get that a lot," Riley chuckled, suddenly at ease again.

Riley and I decided to get moving again because our timers were still counting down. Mine now read 35:13. I wanted to keep talking about the pulses and how Riley knew so much, but I knew my main focus had to still be survival.

We floated aimlessly for miles until we found a cave deep within the water's depths. We approached it and were pleased to find that it was empty. "We should settle here for a while." Riley said. I was hesitant, but eventually I decided he was right. I needed to regain my strength, so I sat down in the cave, utilizing the useful weight of the protective shell around me, put my pack under my right arm, and tried to doze off.

It was dreadfully foggy now. I didn't know where I had ended up, or what I was doing, but I was no longer underwater. Riley wasn't with me either. I closed my eyes and when I opened them, there they were, the pulses within Arena Three. Just like in Arena One, they were beautiful. There were five podiums made of ice. Each podium had a small orb resting on its surface. I stared at them all, wondering which might become mine. I could feel myself greedily reaching for the Freeze Pulse, but when I made contact with it, my arm felt numb. I had the same reaction to the other four pulses as well; they all rejected me.

I couldn't see anything anymore. The whole world seemed to have collapsed when all of a sudden, I heard voices ringing through the air. They were unrecognizable, but they were harsh. "Giving up is what you do, Xavier! Stop trying, and let the world decide your fate!" "Forget confidence and regain fear!" "Death was for you, Xavier, but now you've become mixed up with this Riley boy. Your destiny has changed! You never should have met!"

At that I shot up. A feeling of unexpected shock coursed through me now. I hadn't collected anything. A voice within my head had just completely overpowered me. I held my chest, where my beating heart felt like it wanted to explode. I shook my head violently and sprawled out across the cave's floor, trying to calm my breathing and remember that all I'd experienced was a bad dream.

I clutched at the sand now cushioning my body and held it like a lost child would hold a teddy bear. I heard Riley's voice. "Xavier!" I rolled over and looked up at him.

He was standing over me, and I thought I saw a small hint of fear in his big eyes. Perhaps he was afraid of me dying? Was that possible? Did Riley actually feel some sort of connection with me? I pondered the thought. That seemed to show, in a nutshell, that there was a reason for our meeting, and we had created a bond. I pushed the dream's message out of my head. It was only a dream—how could that be connected to anything real? There was no way to change one's destiny, because everything that happened was in line with destiny. Riley and I had met for a reason.

✳ ✳ ✳

Even though I tried to forget it, I kept playing the dream in my head over and over. Why had my subconscious showed me a fake view of the Arena Three pulses and told me that my destiny had changed because I had met Riley? He and I were friends. Honestly, his companionship was the only thing keeping me sane.

I explained the dream to Riley, but he had no further information about it. In fact, he seemed completely uninterested in the topic, so I did not continue talking about it. I knew it was only a dream, but it seemed so powerful—what more could it be?

10

RILEY'S REVELATION

Riley and I had been half-walking, half-swimming for a while now, and we had found nothing to show us a way to the surface. We had no way of telling if we were even close to our destination, whatever it was. "Riley," I called out. "How are we going to get to the surface?" Riley looked around us as if something might give him the answer. I continued speaking, "This place reminds me of Arena One because there's no destination in sight." Riley shifted uncomfortably at the statement. "What did I say?"

"I'm just...I...I didn't get out of Arena One by myself. I followed someone," Riley murmured.

"What? You know someone else out here? Maybe he can help us!" I exclaimed.

"No," Riley muttered. "He can't because...well...the person I speak of is—you." Riley looked down. I stopped right there when it flooded back to me. All of it. That night! That night I had encountered the pulses...because I had decided to stay up to catch the person who had been eating my dinner roll. I looked at Riley, who wouldn't make eye contact with me.

"You mean, all this time, it was you? You were the one who had eaten my dinner roll that night? You were the one who guided me to the pulses? I never would've found them if I hadn't stayed awake, but you knew that there was a chance that I would stay up to seek out a thief. You mean... was I never meant to find the pulses?" Riley closed his eyes, and he looked ashamed.

Then he started talking. "I—look Xavier, I was alone and scared and tired and...hungry. But more than that, I was desperate. I needed guidance of some sort. But I also needed food. I ate my whole dinner roll on night one, and that was a huge mistake. When I saw you asleep on the desert floor one night, I looked into your pack and had just a tiny bit of your dinner roll. After that, I reread the letter. I knew that if I found the Combat Pulse it would allow my fighting abilities to prosper, and I would stand a chance of survival against the demons in Arena Two. But I was too nervous. I felt as though I had some sort of connection with the Combat Pulse, and I was right, so when I opened the portal into the dimension where the pulses reside, you entered first as my, well, as my what you might call a test-subject. I knew that if you walked out alive, then I would be fine. But seeing that you actually discovered a pulse and it connected with you may mean that I did, in some way, affect your destiny."

I looked at Riley in shock. Had Riley changed my destiny by pushing me to enter the pulse dimension? I looked at him more, and for the first time saw him in a new light. "You never intended to save me in Arena Two, did you?" I asked. "You simply had a debt to pay."

Riley turned around. "I'm sorry," he muttered. "I would've said something, but you being my companion seemed too good too be true, and so I kept it to myself."

I couldn't believe what I was hearing. I wanted to continue confronting Riley, but I glanced at my timer and saw that it read 23:11. That meant I had less than a day now to figure out my survival plan. I refused to say another word and walked right past Riley. He looked up at me, and for the first time, I saw complete, real fear in his eyes.

"Please don't leave me alone," he wailed. I hesitated for a moment but then continued walking, leaving Riley alone in the endless depths of the water.

When I turned back to see if Riley was following me, he was gone.

11

FRIENDS

I couldn't help but wonder where Riley had gone. I stared into the shiny metal blade of my small knife, alone again. I could only see a blurred reflection of my face washing across its surface. I tried to smile into the knife, but the odd reflection made my smile look more like a frown. I rolled it around in my hand.

My timer now read 21:47. I was pressed for time. When I looked at my knife again, it made me realize that I had no apparent need for the thing. It was useless here in the ocean's depths. Even if the High Lord intended for me to use it in self-defense, I didn't think it could get me very far in a fight. I rolled the knife in my hand again. "So then what am I supposed to do with you?" I wondered aloud.

The knife, for some strange reason, seemed to hold the answer that I was looking for. The High Lord wouldn't have just handed me a good old knife unless I could somehow use it to escape these endless waters.

I looked up. There was no sky in sight. I couldn't even see sunlight. The murky water was all that I could see for miles above. That got me thinking.

A hint of a smile wandered across my face as I slowly began to understand exactly how I was going to escape. I raised the knife high, ready to get out of here, but I stopped short of executing my plan. Something inside my gut stopped me. I could feel something tugging on me. Nothing physical—something emotional was holding me back. I looked around. I couldn't figure out what was wrong. Had my dream about the Arena Three pulses affected my ability to escape? A stream of erratic and jumbled thoughts rushed through my head until I figured that something, somewhere, didn't want me to leave here alone. I knew now that I needed to find Riley.

I shoved the knife back into my pack as I rushed through the depths at maximum speed. "Riley!" I yelled. I kept moving. Why I wanted to find him so badly, I could never say, because, frankly, I wasn't all that sure myself. But I moved faster as each second flashed by.

I think I missed my young companion. I knew that what he had done was wrong. He had interfered with my destiny. He had maybe even changed my story forever. But, unfortunately, I couldn't change *that*. I now understood that I could not change the past; it had already happened, so I could not go back to it. But the future was a blank slate; I could control it. I had the power to make whatever I thought impossible possible because I was the ruler of my destiny. Riley might have changed my destiny, but I could now work to further those changes in the best way possible. My first order of business was to ensure that Riley was by my side the entire way.

I kept moving, in a desperate search for my friend. "Riley!" I cried out. He was nowhere to be found. I glanced at my timer, which read 20:55. I had been looking for a very long time, and as soon as time caught up with me, I collapsed.

I flung my body effortlessly into the soft sand beneath my feet. I could feel my heart skip a beat as my lungs blew a fuse. I gasped. Exhaustion had overtaken me. I held my chest now. I was afraid this was my end. I closed my eyes. I thought nothing would get me out of this state of exhaustion. However, I was wrong, for seconds later I heard a loud, mortified shriek of fear that sounded like rocks skidding across a car door. My stomach fizzled as I rose to my feet and bolted toward the sound, with one word keeping me going all that way, even through extreme exhaustion. *Riley*.

I had to cover a lot more distance, and I was almost out of strength when I finally saw something in the distance, something lying on the ground. I trudged toward it with all my might.

When I got closer, I could see the outline of a body.

I hurried as best as I could, and soon my heart skipped yet another beat. It was Riley, and he lay unconscious. His arms were sprawled across his body, and his legs were bent. His forehead was paler than I remembered. The terrible limpness of his body almost made me vomit, but I controlled myself as I stumbled back in shock. All I saw in that moment was my mother, but I quickly forced the thoughts to subside.

As soon as my mind had computed what I was seeing, I rushed to my friend's side. "Riley, no!" I yelled. I shook his motionless body. I touched my fingers to his neck, looking for a pulse.

I waited.

Nothing.

I almost passed out. My friend was not breathing. I flipped him onto his back. "Riley!" I yelled. What could have happened? We had only been separated for a few hours. I looked at him. His features were still, and he showed no signs of life. I could feel a lump forming in my throat. Was he dead? I looked around for anything that could help my friend. I rummaged through my pack and found myself staring at the knife. Perhaps I could follow through with my plan to escape these waters and bring Riley with me, but I couldn't, not yet. My eyes shifted to the one other available object—the Scorch Pulse.

I picked up the pulse, and its warmth rushed through me. I closed my eyes and pictured the Scorch Pulse in my mind. "Please, Scorch Pulse," I whispered. "I beg you to help save my friend." I could only hope. But when I opened my eyes, Riley was still the same.

My eyes settled on his closed ones. I was so over-whelmed. Had I not left him in the first place, this wouldn't have happened.

Then, for the first time, I noticed Riley's pack lying under his arm. Riley wouldn't have had that out if he weren't in dire need of protection. I pulled out the Shadow Pulse and Combat Pulse and then let the pack slip away. I could feel prickles run up my arms now that I had made contact with them. They were not meant to be mine, so they were rejecting me, but I held on as I picked up the Scorch Pulse too. With the power of three pulses, I was sure I could save Riley. I raised the three pulses and begged them for guidance, but I did not possess the strength to hold all three at once, and they sapped my energy, causing me to collapse to the ground once again. All I heard before blacking out was the unsettling sound of glass shattering.

12

TRICKS OF THE TRADE

My eyes fluttered for a moment before I sat up. My muscles were stiff, my legs were jelly, and my arms were cooked noodles. I stood up slowly, in order to keep my balance. It took me a moment to go over everything that had happened before I fell. Then, I remembered.

The three pulses' combined energy must have been too much for me to handle. I took a deep breath before looking down. The pulses were laid out neatly, which was strange, because I could've sworn I heard glass breaking as I fell, or did I imagine it?

I couldn't worry about it right now for two reasons. The first was that Riley still lay on the sand, and the second reason was that my timer now read 12:30.

I pulled Riley to his feet and hooked my arms under his forearms to hold him up, but even for a ten year old, he was heavy. I looked him up and down quickly, wondering what had happened to him. Then, I saw something—something that could have without a doubt caused Riley to scream—his air tank had a long slice in it. All the air had been slowly draining. Something had broken through the shell and cut open the tank, so it was now filling with water. I was shocked that I had missed it before, but of course, I had only examined his body, never his equipment. I would remember that next time.

I quickly picked up the three pulses and placed them in my pack before removing the knife. I stared at it. It was the key to ending this whole nightmare underwater. I looked at Riley and I felt a stab of pity grasp my heart. For the first time, I fully understood that Riley was really only ten. He had so much life ahead of him. But of course, so did I.

"Wish us luck because this is our only hope and...it could be our last," I murmured aloud, with the knowledge that nobody could hear me. I pulled the air tank off of my back and placed it in front of me. I raised the knife and brought it down, jamming it with all my might into the air tank. It took a good thirty seconds, but I pried the top of the air tank off and then quickly flipped it upside down like a rocket. As the air flooded out of it I wrapped one arm around it and gripped one of Riley's wrists to pull him over my shoulder like a sack. The air blasted Riley and me straight up. It was a crazy idea that was filled with risk. I closed my eyes as the pressure increased, as Riley's arm tightened around my neck.

Suddenly, all the air in my tank was gone, and we were only going up because our momentum refused to give out. That was my big mistake: I had not calculated correctly, and this amount of air wouldn't be enough. I was going to lose momentum any minute now and would drown as I floated back to the bottom of the ocean.

Then, suddenly, something grasped my shoulders and began to pull me up. I couldn't see what was pulling me up because the pressure still forced my eyes closed, so I held onto Riley with both hands as we were both pulled to the surface.

Whatever was pulling us up was very fast because my ears were popping like corn kernels.

Then, almost instantly, a vortex appeared.

However, unlike the black-and-green vortexes I'd encountered in the past, this vortex was red and black, making it seem much scarier and more malevolent. I quickly looked up, but I missed seeing whatever had saved us because we were sucked into the vortex. I was sure that something hot stroked my cheek before we disappeared into the coaster of red and black.

When I opened my eyes, the vortex coaster was gone. I looked around to find that I was in a small room. The walls were dark in color and made the room seem tighter.

Behind me, Riley lay up against a wall with both my pack and his own resting against his hip. I was surprised to hear him snoring lightly. He had somehow survived, as if by magic.

I was grateful for whatever made that happen.

But now I had to face my destiny. This was Arena Four, the most feared and dangerous arena of them all, according to the High Lord.

Suddenly, from within the wooden floor beneath me, a small spark frisked its way up into the air before dissipating. Two more sparks were followed by five sparks, and suddenly, a fire sprang up from the floor. However, this fire was much more beautiful than any I'd ever seen. It had a yellow core but the rest was a vibrant shade of sky blue. Its powerful heat rushed over my body and enveloped me in a strange warmth, like a sweater from a stranger.

I stared into the fire, anxious about what would happen next. Arena Four was said to be dangerous, but I was kneeling before a blue fire, my sleeping companion resting only inches away from me.

I felt in no way threatened.

At that thought, the flames engulfed the other end of the room, and I was now able to see my reflection in the blue fire. My hair was a tangled mess, and I was back into my old clothes. These were the clothes that I had been forced to give away when I began my test. But the main purpose of the reflection was clearly not to see my outfit but to see myself.

I stared into my own eyes as the reflection became more real.

I wondered what would happen next, when all of a sudden my reflection popped out of the fire.

The reflection was completely transparent, but otherwise, it looked exactly like me. It spoke with my voice, but it had a metallic undertone to it, so everything it said sounded like it was vibrated out of its mouth rather than being spoken normally.

"Greetings, Xavier. I was honestly not expecting you to show up. It is a true shock that you survived all of the other arenas. You are certainly something special. Your collection of the Scorch Pulse has proven you to be quite powerful and magical at the same time. You see, I am a powerful illusion created by the High Lord called the All-Seeing Celestial, and anything that stares into the fire becomes something that I can mirror so that I may speak with those trying to accomplish their ultimate goal, like you. In other words, when you looked into the fire, I was able to make a copy of you materialize and possess it." The All-Seeing Celestial did not leave any opportunities for an interruption. "You are the first to contact me in years. Now that you *have* contacted me, I can see everything that you've encountered on your journey and before that as well. You do possess skills that would certainly impress the High Lord. However, you are not the worthy one. I won't let you be." The All-Seeing Celestial's voice grew deeper and darker. "The High Lord couldn't catch you in Arena Two where you failed, so now he plans to try again. Don't move!"

Suddenly, the reflection was grasping two metal spears.

It crossed them at my neck in a dangerous position, and I dared not move because I couldn't tell if they were an illusion or not.

I gasped, overwhelmed as I looked back at Riley. Two more reflections of me had appeared and were surrounding my sleeping friend.

We were trapped.

The High Lord had caught up with us, and now we had nowhere to run.

13

THE TRUTH HURTS

My wrists were sore from the tough metal that held them together. At first, I couldn't comprehend what had happened because it was all so unexpected. The High Lord had been waiting for Riley and me all that time since Arena Two. He had set a trap for us in Arena Four. I was very anxious, totally unaware of what my fate would be now.

Riley had awakened. I had missed him more than I could ever put into words, but he was chained not just at the wrists but also at the ankles. I didn't understand why only Riley had been chained at the wrists and the ankles, but I didn't think I would ever know.

Riley seemed to be having a tough time breathing, and he was sweating uncontrollably. All the water he had swallowed had flooded his systems, and frankly, I had no idea how he had survived that. Still, the slice in his tank had been small, so the water probably took a while to collect. I began trying to talk to him. "So, Riley, what happened to you? I mean, before I found you."

Riley seemed very uncomfortable all of a sudden, and he shivered. "I...I was—" Riley choked on his words and took a while to finally put them into a sentence, and even when he did, he seemed uneasy, "You see Xavier, the slice was—it was—I did it! I sliced open my air tank—with my knife." I raised an eyebrow. I knew Riley was daring and strong, but above all I knew that he was not foolish. He dropped his head to avoid eye contact with me.

I instantly knew he was lying.

Riley had never seemed good at lying, but this was downright pathetic.

"Riley, come on. I'm no fool, and I know that you're not, so what really happened to your air tank? I want to know so that we can be cautious of it if we ever see it again."

"Why do you keep saying 'it'?"

"What? Because I have no idea what happened to you."

Riley became silent, lost in thought at what I had just said. He began to breathe loudly, but he shut his mouth instantly when a long sound echoed through the room. It was the sound of a door creaking open reluctantly and slowly as if it hadn't been opened in centuries.

I looked up, and I saw the High Lord approaching us.

He had begun to grow a small, gray moustache, and he had a large purple cape draped over his fancy robes. I bit my lip as I scanned his face. My eyes met those eyes, those same icy eyes that I'd seen at the Relegation Ceremony. I could feel a small chill run up my spine.

Then, the Queen elegantly ambled in. Her hair was held up in a perfectly made bun. I could see her earrings (definitely made of solid gold) and they were frightening. On the left ear was a sword, with shades of red at its tips, and on the right ear was a human skull. She was wearing a dress that was a mixture of sun orange and evening sky pink colors. If not for her gigantic high heels that looked more like weapons than footwear and her shady expression she might have been pretty.

I turned away and faced Riley, who strangely, seemed to be afraid. The High Lord did not scare me. He just overwhelmed me.

He spoke. "Xavier Key and Riley Aurarance, correct? I am surprised that you made it through Arena Three. And only running into my goth demon once? I was pleased that he found you, but I am displeased that he did not kill you. It should have been your last day, Riley, but your new friend Xavier scared my demon off with his powerful connection to the Scorch Pulse, an ancient treasure he never should have found. I wish you had never guided him to the pulse dimension in Arena One. Don't you see? He would be long dead by now if the Scorch Pulse hadn't been supporting him, helping him do smart things. He was your pawn, Riley, but now you're mine, you slimy little nuisance."

Riley looked down as a tear formed in his eye. I was lost. The tension of this all seemed to wrap around us and squeeze us tight.

"He doesn't know, so please stop!" Riley blurted out. I was caught off guard because I had no idea what he meant. I looked at the High Lord, wondering what he'd say.

"My dear boy, I had no intention of giving away personal information, but now seeing that it will cause you great pain, I think I might." The High Lord seemed to enjoy saying these words as they curled off his lips dangerously.

"No! Now is not the time! He'll hate me! Please don't!" Riley yelled desperately. The High Lord looked at Riley, as though he were about to agree, but then the Queen narrowed her eyes and a dark glint flickered in the High Lord's eyes as his mouth rotated from a dissatisfied frown to an evil grin.

"It seems, Xavier, you do not know everything about Riley. Riley is more powerful than you know. He possesses strengths and weaknesses that I myself harbor. But what is that phrase? The apple doesn't fall from the tree! Yes, that's it." The High Lord paused, his eyes glittering. "I hope this has been a most telling conversation. Your execution will be completed soon. When the guards come, you'll know that it's time. Nice knowing you," the High Lord said sarcastically as he whirled around and began to stroll out, but I noticed out of the corner of my eye that he flinched before exiting for good.

I stared at Riley in disbelief. If I had pieced everything the High Lord had just said together correctly, then that would mean...

"The High Lord is your father!" Riley looked down, clearly ashamed. I continued raging. "You didn't think I needed to know that? Man, Riley, it's just one secret after the next with you, huh? I can't believe I thought we were friends. What else are you hiding? Just say it. It seems I'll find out anyway."

"I knew you'd hate me if you found out." Riley murmured.

I just about exploded. "I don't hate you because the High Lord's your father, Riley. I hate you because you kept it from me all this time. I hate you because you think you're my superior. I hate you because you can't just be an honest friend to me. I hate you because you're just like your father: power-hungry, secretive, and a complete jerk!" I was fuming, but Riley didn't get a chance to respond because the guards showed up and took us away. All was lost, and everything would soon be over for me. The feelings I'd had at the Relegation Ceremony had begun all over again.

14

UNDERSTANDING THE PUZZLE

The plan for our execution was explained to us in very little detail. The High Lord had designed a giant arena—not another elementally enhanced one, a regular battlefield—where Riley and I would be forced to face off against his goth demon. I knew his plan was to have his demon kill us in the fight, making our death only that much more painful for us and more enjoyable for him.

We walked into the arena, still tangled in chains. The guards gave us both a shove through the large doors, and we stumbled in. The entire arena was a giant circle, and there were large bleachers all around. The High Lord along with many subjects sat on those bleachers.

The Queen however did not make an appearance.

The ground beneath us was soft, like the desert sand in Arena One. I stared around hopelessly, knowing that I had no chance of survival. Then the goth demon leapt through the door behind us and snarled, prepared to show no mercy.

The goth demon was huge. It had a dog-like face with large fangs, a pointed nose, and two blood-red eyes. Its long, slim body was wrapped in black fur with small spikes jutting out of it all over. The goth demon also had a swinging tail with a large point at the end of it. I staggered back in utter fear like a true coward. Riley seemed more terrified than me, but I still felt no reason to try and comfort him. I hated him now.

Suddenly the demon leapt into the air and revealed four paws with razor-sharp claws jutting out of them. One of those paws swiped at Riley, sending him flying into a wall and leaving him dazed. I shuddered and began to run around the demon, trying to confuse it, but it seemed to be very smart and whacked me with its long tail, sending me flying.

I had never been hit so hard or sent so far.

The pain I felt when I bashed into the wall was extraordinary, like getting hit with a bus three times. I could feel a pool of saliva slip off my lip and drip down my face. I coughed in reaction to having the wind knocked out of me.

That was when I looked up and saw the demon's giant fangs rushing at me with tremendous speed. I closed my eyes, and my life flashed before me, but the demon never hit me. "No!" I heard the High Lord scream. I waited a moment and then, when nothing happened, I risked opening my eyes.

At first, I thought that Riley had saved me, but I was wrong.

Levitating in the air before my eyes was the Scorch Pulse.

The streaks that so beautifully ran through it were glowing brighter than usual. And then I noticed the demon lying motionless on the ground. Its tongue was curled over its nose, and its tail was wrapped up as if the creature felt fear. I stared at the creature first with pity and then with disgust.

Had the Scorch Pulse saved me? I looked at it as it glowed feverishly. However, I did not have time to admire its beauty because an arrow slipped past my face.

I whipped around to find hundreds of archers aiming their arrows and loosing them at me. I ducked and spun and jumped to avoid the fast-flying arrows, and then a large wave of fire rushed past me and completely disintegrated the remaining arrows—and the archers firing them. I again whipped around to face the Scorch Pulse, which was shaking softly.

It was all so strange. This had never before happened.

I glanced at Riley who had long cuts running across his face. A cut even ran across his left eyelid. He was sitting on the ground with his back against a wall, and he looked very weak. Five arrows were lodged in his skin: he had two stuck in his legs, one in his stomach, one in his right arm, and one in his right hand. I could feel a pain within me grow again. I suppressed it and ignored Riley, even though my hate for him was equal to my pity now.

I turned my attention to the Scorch Pulse again. I walked toward it cautiously and let it drop into my hands.

It was warm and felt strong in my hands. In that moment, I felt like it was just the Scorch Pulse and I alone.

It was like I had found the key to something.

I could feel a surge of heat run through my body, and the Scorch Pulse seemed to grow heavier. Right at that moment everything stopped. The world froze before me, and everything flashed away, leaving me in an endless room of light.

The Scorch Pulse levitated into the air and began to whirl around. My hair was frazzled by the powerful wind the spinning pulse was creating. And then, with the spinning, came a powerful, radiant heat. I stepped back a bit in confusion and amazement. Then the Scorch Pulse rushed through the air and began to twist around me like a tornado, surrounding me in a veil of red-orange light.

The Scorch Pulse made contact with my body, and I saw everything. Every question I'd asked was answered. It was as if the Scorch Pulse was enlightening me with its hidden powers. Uncountable images ran through my head, completing the puzzle entirely.

I could see the Relegation Ceremony that I'd attended in my head, but now the picture was clearer. I could see now that on that day so many days ago, the High Lord had never been glaring at me. He had in fact been glaring at the young boy cowering behind me—Riley. I could hear the High Lord whispering to his queen. "Riley is on the list now," he had said. "Should I take him off? This is our last chance to change our minds. He could become powerful and be our ally. What do you think?" And I saw her shake her head, throwing away her last chance to save her son.

Then I saw Riley being viciously attacked by the goth demon underwater.

Following that, I saw myself asleep in that cave, and the Scorch Pulse was glowing inside my pack. It had been communicating with me through a dream.

And then, I saw the moment when Riley and I had been rocketing up to the surface. Now I knew that the Scorch Pulse had actually been lifting us. The heat that I had felt when we were rushing towards the surface had been the Scorch Pulse's warm energy.

Suddenly, I came across something important. The High Lord was alone in a room within his palace. He had flat, bony cheeks and his eyes were glazed. He seemed to be much younger than he was today, but his mind was clearly set on something. The walls and decorations were fuzzy, but they were not important at the moment. The High Lord was waving his hands in unison and spinning them strangely. A long, ruby-colored line twisted out of the air in front of his spinning hands and began to weave a large door. I instantly recognized the door. It was the same caramel door from the day I'd been banished. The High Lord began to utter words that I could not understand: *uthshimer shathena bhuckdai.* The ruby line began to widen and two lines split out of it, one green and one black. The lines worked as one to weave the door and its interior. When the door was complete, the lines fused together once more and disappeared into the air. The High Lord dropped to his knees, and I realized that he was doused in sweat, but he stood up and walked toward the door. He slid it open and revealed the vortex, the one that I had encountered. This must have been the day of the very first Relegation Ceremony.

The High Lord was the creator of the arenas and their power and the vortexes.

He controlled everything.

He was an enchanter.

The Scorch Pulse suddenly dropped back into my hands, and the powerful images disappeared. I blinked several times, and the world returned to the exact same scene as when I left it. I now understood that Riley was much more than what he seemed, and he was certainly his father's son, but not by choice.

I raced to Riley's side.

15

A FAMILY OF ENCHANTERS

Riley's skin was stone cold. I shook his body, but for fear of pushing the arrows in more, stopped. I didn't know what to do for him, so I tried to dislodge one of the arrows, but it was stuck in his skin and I did not possess the strength to remove it alone.

Then, a large hand grabbed my shoulder and threw me aside like I was nothing more than an old potato skin.

It was the High Lord.

He laid Riley down flat on the ground. Then he closed his eyes and uttered an enchantment. *"Shathena marsilen yuveta ira."* The words blended together beautifully, like the perfect smoothie ingredients mixing together, and suddenly Riley, the High Lord, and I teleported away from the arena in an instant.

We reappeared in a room. The room was small, like an office, and along each wall was a wooden shelf, and on each shelf were five indentations, twenty in all, small alcoves that I inferred were intended to hold something spherical.

The High Lord raised his hands above his head and yelled, *"Asper lireses myocen uit hithsenfire rulthion."* As the words were spoken, each indentation on each shelf was filled with a small orb—each indentation, that is, except for three.

The High Lord had just summoned the other seventeen pulses.

I stared in amazement. The High Lord walked over to the pulses and picked up five of them. He did not collapse as I had when I touched multiple pulses. I recognized each pulse instantly due to the knowledge the Scorch Pulse had given me: the Air Pulse, Freeze Pulse, Water Pulse, Heat Pulse, and Poison Pulse.

The High Lord put his hand to Riley's forehead and murmured something under his breath. Quickly, he picked up the Water Pulse and the Heat Pulse and put them next to Riley's pale temples. The pulses began to glow like disco balls before, somehow, slipping into Riley's head.

When I say the pulses melted into Riley's head and disappeared inside of him, I am not exaggerating.

Suddenly, color returned to Riley's face, and the pulses magically returned to their shelves.

Then, the High Lord took the Air Pulse and laid it on his son's slowly moving chest, and then he placed the Freeze Pulse on his son's stomach. Instantly, upon feeling their powers, Riley's eyes shot open like he had just had a large helping of coffee, and he cringed at the pain of the arrows still lodged within him.

Now it was the Poison Pulse's turn. The High Lord picked up the dark violet orb and said, "*Ilthsinthin.*" At this command, the Poison Pulse levitated into the air and released a deep blue liquid that covered the arrows and somehow removed them from Riley's body and made them disappear. Then it returned to its spot on the Arena Four shelf.

Riley shuddered. Then he sat up and cradled his head in his hands. "What happened to me? I feel like I was run over by a bulldozer."

I spoke up now. "You were knocked out by the force of the arrows back in the arena."

"Arrows?"

"Yeah. Remember? We were attacked by archers when my Scorch Pulse stopped the goth demon?" I gave the High Lord a dark look.

"All I remember is that giant creature slapping me into a wall before blacking out, but it's all still fuzzy. Maybe I have a slight concussion."

The High Lord interrupted. "Riley and Xavier, we must flee now. My enchantment will only protect us here for a short time. Come now." I looked at Riley and tipped my head. He returned the glance, a distant look in his eyes, and then he turned to his father and nodded in agreement.

"Xavier, before we do anything, I want to tell you my biggest secret, so that you never have doubts about our friendship again. My father is an enchanter, a being with the power to use magic and spells to create or reveal things. An enchanter can also pass on his teachings. So, I am also an enchanter and can call forth magic powers when necessary, but usually I refrain from using them. You, Xavier, are also an enchanter, though you may not know it."

"What? I'm not an enchanter. I can't use magic."

"You can though. Didn't the Scorch Pulse show you images of the past? Aren't things clearer now?"

"Yes but—"

"Well then, that is magic. The Scorch Pulse is what will give you your magic. Remember when you had the awful nightmare, back in Arena Three? What you were hearing was the Scorch Pulse piecing together recent and future events so that you could see them. It's strange, but you'll understand soon."

I was in awe at the revelation.

I was an enchanter!

Or at least Riley claimed I was. This was the first I'd ever heard the term used to describe me. It was all very exciting, but the High Lord interrupted our conversation.

"Riley, you'll have to explain the rest of how an enchanter's magic works later. Now, we must flee. The Queen, she will be coming for us." He grabbed Riley's wrist and my arm and quickly uttered a spell. "*Rily rily tily uit tily juli-hiu vy.*" The room around us disappeared, and I could feel a strong wind gust rush against my face as we flew through space and time.

Suddenly, we landed on solid ground, and the High Lord ushered Riley and me before him. I didn't know where we were. It felt like an abandoned beach area, but the ground was soil, not sand, and whatever water had been there was reduced to some small pools of muck. Behind us, there were large boulder masses.

We entered an alcove between two of the big boulders, so it felt like a small cave. The High Lord knelt on the ground and gestured for us to do the same, so we did. He spoke.

"Please Riley, I'd like to explain to Xavier so that we can complete this as soon as possible." Riley nodded. "Xavier, you must understand the most crucial issue we face. I am not the one in control. You see, it is my Queen who is indirectly in charge. She works as High Lord through me using enchantments to influence my words, actions, and thoughts. She is very sinister and will stop at nothing to achieve her goal of eliminating the male portion of our species forever. Everything you've ever seen me do was in fact the Queen working my body like a puppet. I am her puppet. She wants Riley dead, and soon, she will feel the same way about you. The only reason that I'm alive today is so that she can continue her rule through me. It is challenging to make this sound believable, but she will destroy me if I rebel against her, so I avoid the thought as much as possible. She is a more skilled enchanter than even I. I understand that this is all very abrupt and confusing, but you must know that I am using a protection spell to block out the Queen's influence right now, so this is no lie. I am on your side when I am me." I stared at the High Lord in awe. At first, I thought this was all a trap, but when I looked into his eyes, I noticed that they were not icy anymore. They were warm and apologetic.

"I guess I believe you. What has telling me helped you with though?"

"You are the key, Xavier. That is what helps. You are the next High Lord."

I was dumbfounded. "Wait! What? No no, my mother had no relationship to you as far as I know, and as you also know, I don't have a father. I came from the Pool of Life, like all children do on our island. It's not possible."

"But it is. You see, it is not blood that decides who will be the next High Lord. The High Lord decides himself. I have chosen you. Your connection to the Scorch Pulse, which was not predestined, proves to me that you are the one. However, today is not the day that you will claim the throne. Today, I am forced to ask you to do something for me."

Without warning, the cave tumbled in on us before the High Lord could continue. I could feel the heavy weight of the ceiling crush me with the force of a rampaging elephant. When the dust slithered away, I coughed and pushed my way up through the rubble. Riley and the High Lord did the same.

I was covered in dust and soot. I looked up and saw the Queen standing a few meters away with a smug expression on her face. Behind her was a moderate pack of vicious darkness demons, as if she didn't expect their job to require many numbers. I stood up and looked at her intensely, prepared to say something witty, but she spoke first.

"Xavier Key, Riley Aurarance, and my High Lord, how surprising to find you all in one place." The Queen began studying her nails, as if this conversation was almost boring to her. "It is also surprising to see that you all survived getting crushed, no matter though, so let me get right to the point. I want you to leave my island now—but certainly not alive. *Hithsenfire rouble!*" The Queen's spell crafted two gigantic fireballs out of mid-air and then they were launched at us.

The High Lord stood in front of the rubble the cave-in had created and held out his hands yelling, "*Joonju!*" A large, stone, wall-like barrier formed before us, and the Queen's fireballs crashed into it but couldn't break through, although they did not de-materialize, instead they kept trying to break it down. The High Lord looked like he had just run a marathon while carrying a cow, but he shouted, "Quickly, Xavier and Riley, get behind something heavy!"

Riley and I crawled behind a very large chunk of boulder created by the cave's destruction. "That spell she used, it is the strongest fire spell known to enchanters," Riley murmured. "I don't know how long he can hold it off."

I noticed that Riley referred to his parents as "he" and "she" rather than father and mother, but I couldn't worry about it right now.

"Riley, help the High Lord," I insisted. Riley hesitated, but then he stood up and uttered a spell. "*Hithsenfire ororanch!*"

Suddenly, the fireballs exploded, sending us all tumbling backward. Riley landed on top of me, and the High Lord landed a few feet away from us. The Queen was sent tumbling backward as well and landed with a thud.

The fire destroyed all of the darkness demons before they could get to us. I shook my head and stood up, followed by Riley and the High Lord, who rose slowly.

We walked over to the Queen who looked like she was having a dream about murdering all of her enemies with her eyes shut and a wicked grin running across her face. The High Lord pulled her to her feet, but didn't startle her. She did not seem the least bit frightened as she opened her dark eyes. She scowled at us as if to say *go away peasants*. Riley chuckled briefly and looked at her, his sights obviously set on a little revenge.

"I hope you suffer the way you wanted our son to," the High Lord murmured. The Queen's lip quivered, but she did not respond, and I couldn't tell if she was feigning sadness or not.

The High Lord uttered a spell. *"Lorislyth xycer rifer."*

The caramel door that housed the entrance to the arenas suddenly appeared. Riley twisted the knob and pulled it open, revealing the green and black portal to a place that no one ever wanted to go.

The Queen gasped and mouthed something, but I couldn't read her lips.

Then, the High Lord thrust the Queen inside yelling, "Good luck if you are truly worthy! And if not, then may you find peace with death!"

Then she was gone.

EPILOGUE

After banishing the Queen into the arenas forever, the High Lord destroyed all remaining vortexes with an enchantment, which meant that the Queen would have no way back to the islands and soon she would perish.

A few days later, Riley, the High Lord, and I met at the palace, where I was now an occasional resident. We were in what the High Lord called the living room. We sat on large, plush, red couches. The room was huge and a lot of strange art lined the sky blue walls. A giant chandelier that was wrapped in diamonds hung from the ceiling, offering warm light.

The High Lord explained to us that a close friend of his had contacted him and said that a danger had surfaced on another island, so his immediate attention was required. He would have to leave our island and investigate.

For the time being, Riley and I would be in control of the island. We would have to make sure that no crimes were committed and that the High Lord's duties were fulfilled. I was excited to be a true leader for once, but the High Lord explained more.

"Xavier," He began, "I think you should start to learn basic enchanting while I am away. Riley will tutor you and there are a number of hardcover books in a chest upstairs that you can use. The Scorch Pulse will assist you and help you learn faster."

"Cool!" I exclaimed. "I can't wait to be able to control enchantments."

"There's more." The High Lord added quickly. "I would also like Riley to teach you the language of the ancients, which is the writing on the plaques in the pulse dimensions."

"Why does he have to learn that language? Almost no one uses it these days." Riley implored.

The High Lord raised his eyebrows and gave Riley an annoyed look that said *please let me finish*! "Let me explain why knowing that language is important." The High Lord's annoyed expression did not agree with his sophisticated, mannered tone. "The threat that I am going to investigate... I shouldn't say too much about it as there is no confirmation that anything is true. But, I can tell you that I do not know exactly what I am dealing with. If I don't return in thirty days, I want you to unlock this." The High Lord handed Riley a small scroll that was locked in a small, transparent case. "The case can only be unlocked with an enchantment in thirty days. Inside is something that will... help us stay in contact if necessary, but hopefully it will not need to be opened."

"What does all of that have to do with me learning the language of the ancients?" I asked.

"Xavier, you have much to learn. To answer your question, you will understand why you must know it when the time comes. But for now, you must understand that if this danger is overwhelming, I will need your help. Both of you." I could tell that the High Lord was very much against putting me in harm's way, not to mention his own son, but I understood.

"If you are not back in thirty days, we *are* coming after you." I said courageously.

"We enchanters have to stick together." Riley added.

The High Lord smiled approvingly, and then Riley left to go to the market. As I stood up to leave after him, the High Lord gave me a look.

I stared at him and realized that the coldness in his eyes was gone, which relieved me.

But, for a split second, the High Lord's eyes flashed a deep golden color. "And so it begins." He murmured, golden eyed. Then, his eyes switched back to normal, and he got up, slowly walking away as if nothing had happened at all.

The High Lord soon departed for his voyage, leaving Riley and me to tend to the island. I was very distracted about what had transpired between the High Lord and me in his living room, but I tried to stay focused. I'd decided not to tell Riley about it either because, frankly, the poor kid had enough on his mind. It was hard to stay focused, but I managed to start learning basic enchanting.

Within only a few days, I was beginning to become a strong enchanter, but it was hard work. The first enchantment Riley taught me was *"Hithsenfire!"* which basically meant fire. I liked the way the word felt as I spoke it, but I wasn't sure why.

That evening, the lights in my room died, leaving me in a shroud of darkness. I was excited at the opportunity to test my power as a rookie enchanter. Carefully, I flexed my left hand.

"Hithsenfire," I chanted.

A small spark suddenly formed on my palm. It danced around for a moment and let me eye the dark room, but I could not have cared less about the room at that point.

I'd created fire!

It fizzled out pretty quickly though. I stared at my now-empty palm—which was not burned or even tanned—and said aloud, "One day I will be the strongest enchanter to live, and I will claim my throne to make the world a better place than it ever was, starting with this island. I will turn our island into a paradise—a place where people can enjoy themselves. Somewhere that people can really call home."

I sat down on the bed and then swung under the large sheets and rested against the soft pillow. Soon, my eyes became heavy and I closed them, lulled to sleep by my thirst for tomorrow and the heat that now constantly swam through my veins.

ENCHANTMENT TRANSLATIONS

U thshimer shathena bhuckdai (Us-shy-murr shu-then-ah buck-die): Bring a power to teleport/Teleport

Shathena marsilen yuveta ira (Shu-then-ah mars-isle-in you-vet-ah ear-ah): Go to a secret room of magic

Asper lireses myocen uit hithsenfire rulthion (As-per lyre-seas my-oh-chin oot highs-then-fire rule-thee-on): Earth, air, water, and fire appear

Ilthsinthin (Illth-sin-thin): Heal/Fix/Aid

Rily rily tily uit tily juli-hiu vy (Rily rily tily oot tily july-hue v): Two young males and me transport away

Hithsenfire rouble (Highs-then-fire rue-bull): Fire doubles/Doubled fire power

Joonju (June-jew): Protection enchantment/Shield

Hithsenfire ororanch (Highs-then-fire aura-ranch): Fire explosion/Exploding fire

Lorislyth xycer rifer (Loris-lith zi-sir rye-fur): Appear element vortex

Hithsenfire (Highs-then-fire): Fire

Book 2
The Continued Story of Xavier Key
Coming Soon

Matthew Albren is a young author already achieving his dreams at the age of twelve. An exceptional student, he enjoys school and is committed to making good grades and even better impressions. After practicing karate for four years and tennis for almost a year, he now devotes his physical energy to playing soccer.

Albren hasn't won any official writing awards—yet—but he's earned an A+ on every school writing assignment for as far back as he can remember. His story *The World of Gadzooks*, later renamed *The World of Gazvolt*, was posted on a viral news website. His latest work of fiction, *Survival of the Elements*, is the beginning of a dystopian fantasy series set in the world of young Xavier Key.

Albren lives in Massachusetts with his parents and his younger brother.

Made in the USA
Middletown, DE
24 November 2015